DORRIE
and the
Halloween Plot
by Patricia Coombs

Lothrop, Lee & Shepard Company

A Division of William Morrow & Company, Inc.

New York

Other books by Patricia Coombs

Dorrie and the Amazing Magic Elixir

Dorrie and the Birthday Eggs

Dorrie and the Blue Witch

Dorrie and the Fortune Teller

Dorrie and the Goblin

Dorrie and the Haunted House

Dorrie and the Weather-Box

Dorrie and the Witch Doctor

Dorrie and the Witch's Imp

Dorrie and the Wizard's Spell

Lisa and the Grompet

Molly Mullett

Mouse Café

Library of Congress Cataloging in Publication Data
Coombs, Patricia.
   Dorrie and the Halloween plot.
   SUMMARY: Dorrie, the little witch, foils the plan of the Halloween demons to kidnap the Great Sorceress and steal the Book of Shadows, and is rewarded by a promise of flying lessons from the Great Sorceress herself.
   [1. Witches—Fiction. 2. Halloween—Fiction]
I. Title.
PZ7.C7813Dkp   [Fic]   76-3643
ISBN 0-688-41764-7   ISBN 0-688-51764-1 lib. bdg.

For ANN and TRISH

This is Dorrie. She is a witch. A little witch. Her
hat is always on crooked and her socks don't match.
She lives with her mother, the Big Witch, and Cook.
Wherever Dorrie goes, her black cat, Gink, goes
with her.

One Friday Dorrie jumped out of bed. She did a
somersault. "Gink," said Dorrie, "it's Halloween!
Last Halloween Mother said she'd give me a flying
lesson *this* Halloween!"

Dorrie skipped down the hall. She slid down the banister. She ran into the kitchen. Gink went with her.

"Happy Halloween, Cook!" shouted Dorrie. "Today I get a flying lesson!"

"SHHH!" said Cook, crossly. "I have pumpkin cake in the oven."

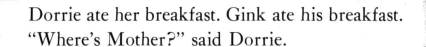

Dorrie ate her breakfast. Gink ate his breakfast. "Where's Mother?" said Dorrie.

"In the sewing room. She's working on our costumes for the Halloween Pageant," said Cook.

Dorrie skipped down the hall, and Gink went with her. They went into the sewing room. The Big Witch was sitting beside an old trunk. Stuff was piled all around her.

"Happy Halloween!" said Dorrie. "I'm all ready for my first flying lesson. Shall I take the broomstick out to the front yard?"

"Flying lesson? Broomstick?" The Big Witch frowned. "What are you talking about? You're too young to fly. Maybe next year. Your costume is almost ready to try. . . ."

"You said I could learn to fly THIS Halloween. You said you were too busy LAST Halloween. I'm always too young when you're too busy. I'll NEVER learn to fly!" said Dorrie.

"Shhh!" cried the Big Witch. "I'm too busy. You know we're giving a Pageant for the Great Sorceress. It's all planned. Everyone has worked very hard on it. The Halloween Demons are coming to put on an Air Show. The brass band from Mushollow is coming to play. And Witchville is putting on the Pageant."

Dorrie sighed. "What am I going to be?"

"You're going to be a little princess. Cook is going to be a castle and I'm. . . ."

"A LITTLE PRINCESS! Oh, no!" cried Dorrie.

"Stand still! You're too old to make such a fuss,"
said the Big Witch. "This is the costume. I wore it
in a Pageant for the Sorceress. I once took lessons
in magic from her. She is the greatest and oldest
sorceress in the whole of Witchdom. She is keeper
of the Book of Shadows. Every magic recipe in the
world is in the Book of Shadows."

"Every single one?" said Dorrie.

The Big Witch turned pink, then red. "Not quite. One is missing. I lost it, a long time ago."

"Was the Great Sorceress mad? I bet she was. Tell me about it."

"NO!" snapped the Big Witch. "Not now." She pulled the costume over Dorrie's head.

"Perfect!" cried the Big Witch. "Now, the mask."
Dorrie looked in the mirror and frowned. The
mask smiled sweetly. Dorrie groaned. Gink yawned.

"I hate it," said Dorrie. "I feel like a dummy."

"Never mind how you feel," said the Big Witch. "You look like a princess and you must act like one. We're going outside to practice. I'll teach you how to curtsy."

All morning the Big Witch and Cook and Dorrie practiced. Everything went fine, except the curtsies. Every time Dorrie curtsied, her feet got mixed up and she fell down.

The Big Witch was getting crosser and crosser. Dorrie was getting crosser and crosser. Cook went inside to ice the cake.

"It's this dumb costume," said Dorrie. "If I didn't have to wear all these silly skirts, I could do it."

"You DO have to wear them," yelled the Big Witch. "Go have lunch. Then practice until you can do it RIGHT. I have to put on my knight costume. Then I have to go help Squig and Mr. Obs with their costumes. You go with Cook. I'll meet you at the Manor."

After lunch Dorrie and Gink went back outside. Dorrie tried another curtsy. She landed on her back.

The front door slammed. The Big Witch rushed out.

"I'm late, I must hurry!" said the Big Witch. "Oh, I forgot to tell Cook you're going with her. Tell her I'll meet you both there. Drat! I have the wrong broomstick. Run get my other one for me."

Dorrie ran and got the Big Witch's best broomstick. The Big Witch handed Dorrie her old one. "Now get those curtsies RIGHT!" said the Big Witch. And she flew away over the treetops.

Dorrie sighed. "Come on, Gink, we'll go over in the field to practice. I don't want anybody to see me looking like this until I have to."

Into the field they went. Dorrie practiced and practiced. Gink took a nap in the grass. It got later and later.

"At last! I can do it!" said Dorrie. "If I keep my left foot from stepping on the hem, I don't fall over."

Dorrie heard something. She looked up. The brass band from Mushollow flew over them on the way to the Manor.

"Gink, look! Way over there, the Halloween Demons! Oh, I wish we were in the Air Show. We'd do loop-the-loops and figure eights just like they're doing."

The Demons dropped behind the trees.

"Hmm," said Dorrie. "I was SO busy, I forgot to put away this old broomstick. Let's try a little flying all by ourselves. It would be a nice surprise for Mother."

Dorrie got on the broomstick. Gink got on behind her. Dorrie gave a kick and whispered: "Shooma, shooma, shoom!" The broomstick slowly rose into the air. Another kick, another whisper, and they went a little higher.

"Gink, we're flying! We're really flying! It's easy!"

All at once the broomstick began to spin around and around. With every spin it flew faster. Higher and higher it went, spinning faster and faster.

Dorrie kicked one foot, then the other. She kicked both feet. She said all the magic words she knew. Nothing worked. The broomstick kept on spinning, up and up and up.

Slowly the broomstick stopped spinning. It began to bounce up and down. It flipped upside down, and took off full speed. Down into Witchville it swooped. Zigging and zagging, it whizzed around roofs and chimneys like a rocket.

"Hang on, Gink, we're going to crash!" yelled
Dorrie, as the broomstick shot through backyards.
It sailed smack into a clothesline, flipped around,
and sped back up into the air. High up over the
trees and houses they flew, the wet clothes flapping
wildly.

Dorrie tried to turn the broomstick. She leaned to the left. She leaned to the right. The broomstick went full speed ahead, straight for the Town Tower.

"Oh, no!" said Dorrie. She pulled back hard on the broomstick. They whizzed so close to the tower all the bats flew out. The clothesline caught on the tower, and the broomstick swung around and around and around. The clothesline snapped. They shot off through the air.

In a few seconds they were out of Witchville and back over the field again. The broomstick slowed down. It began to bounce and spin again, around and around. "We've got to get down from here," said Dorrie. "I'm so dizzy I can't remember what Mother says to make it land. Something like KIMONA, KAMOO, or KAROON, KAREE. . . ."

The broomstick stopped. It bounced a little. All at once it flew full speed straight down, whizzing closer and closer to the ground. Down, down, down they went, flying straight for Black Pond.

There was a splash and a whish. The broomstick dragged Dorrie and Gink through the water. Dorrie pulled back on the handle. They shot out of the water, up into a tree, and stopped.

"My first landing," said Dorrie.

Gink shook the water out of his fur. Dorrie looked at her costume. It was gray and soggy. The curls hanging from the mask were limp and gray. Dorrie reached up to take the mask off. She pulled. She tugged.

"This dumb mask has SHRUNK and wrinkled up. It won't come off. Gink, we're in trouble. When Mother sees this mess, I'll be sent to my room forever."

It was getting darker and darker. Dorrie's house looked small and far away. Something moved in the yard, then rose into the air.

"There's Cook!" said Dorrie. "She'll come and find us. No, she won't. I never did tell her I was going with her. She thinks I'm at the Pageant."

Dorrie sat in the tree, dripping and thinking. She heard sounds. "Someone's coming!" she said. "They'll help us get out of here and over to the Manor."

The voices grew louder. Dorrie looked down through the branches. It was the Halloween Demons. Dorrie called. They were too busy talking to hear her.

"This is the plan," said one of them, drawing with a stick in the dirt. "The Manor is here. The old lady will be alone on the balcony with the Book of Shadows beside her. All the others are down below.

"Zane, Zeke, and Zeno put on an Air Show like these yokels have never seen before. Everybody is looking at the Air Show. There's a tower beside the balcony. Zip and I will hide behind it until you three start setting off fireworks.

"When the fireworks start, Zip and I fly to the balcony. I grab the old lady. Zip grabs the Book of Shadows. Then it's back to the cave, full speed."

Zane, Zeke, and Zeno frowned. "We need a head start. They'll be after us in a flash. We have to get the old lady locked up in the cave before they catch up."

Zed scowled. "Fly FAST. We can do it. As long as we have the old lady, they won't do anything to us."

They leaped on their broomsticks. Whiz, whiz, whiz, whiz, whiz, they flew into the air.

Dorrie held very still in the top of the tree. "Gink," she whispered, "a plot to kidnap the Sorceress! We've got to. . . ."

Whiz, whiz, whiz, whiz, whiz—the Demons came back again, flying around the tree.

"It's just some old rags," yelled Zeno. "An old dummy or scarecrow blown out of the fields. Come on, let's go."

"Wait!" yelled Zed. "It's just what we need! We'll put the dummy in place of the old lady. Nobody will know it's a dummy until AFTER the Pageant. By then we'll be back at the cave."

"Zed's right!" shouted Zip. "Grab the dummy!"

"Quick, Gink," whispered Dorrie. "Go find the Big Witch!" Gink slid down the tree and ran.

The Demons grabbed Dorrie. They tied her to Zip's broomstick, and off they flew.

Over the fields and houses, over the Town Tower, on and on they flew.

"We'll split up now," called Zed. "Zip and I will fly in from the back while you three fly in from the front."

Behind the tower near the balcony, Zip and Zed landed on a narrow sill. They untied Dorrie and dumped her down between them.

Dorrie heard voices and music and clapping. Trumpets blared. A drum rolled. And over the court-yard the three Halloween Demons began their Air Show.

Out front there were shouts and cries, OOOHHHs and AAAHHHs as the flying Demons did figure eights and leapfrogs. They hung from their knees from the broomsticks, they did handstands and head-stands. They rode on each other's shoulders. The witches and wizards clapped and cheered.

BOOM! The flying Demons set off the fire-works. Fireworks whizzed and whirled over the Manor.

"Now!" cried Zip, grabbing Dorrie around the middle.

"Ready!" cried Zed.

Down to the balcony they swooped. As Zed grabbed the Great Sorceress and lifted her up, Zip dumped Dorrie into the chair.

In a flash, Dorrie reached up and grabbed the Great Sorceress by the ankles and kicked Zip away from the Book of Shadows.

"We've been tricked," grunted Zip. "It was a spy, not a dummy!"

"Get the Book, get the Book!" shouted Zed, trying to pull the Sorceress away from Dorrie.

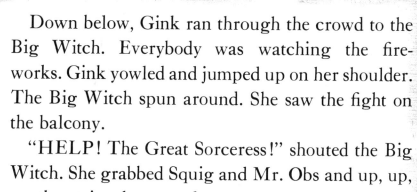

Down below, Gink ran through the crowd to the Big Witch. Everybody was watching the fireworks. Gink yowled and jumped up on her shoulder. The Big Witch spun around. She saw the fight on the balcony.

"HELP! The Great Sorceress!" shouted the Big Witch. She grabbed Squig and Mr. Obs and up, up, up the stairs they raced.

High in the air Zane and Zeke and Zeno set off the last three rockets. As the sparks faded away, they saw the fight. With a roar they swooped down.

Dorrie hung on to the Great Sorceress and kept kicking at Zip. The Demons and the Big Witch and Mr. Obs and Squig fought all around her in a wild scramble.

Gink leaped on Zed's back and dug in his claws.

Zed shrieked. He let go of the Great Sorceress. The Sorceress landed on top of Dorrie.

Zip knocked Squig down and got the Book of Shadows. He scrambled up on the railing and got on his broomstick.

"The Book of Shadows!" yelled Dorrie.

As Zip leaped into the air, Squig grabbed the end of the broomstick. Dorrie grabbed Squig. The Great Sorceress grabbed Dorrie. The Big Witch grabbed the Great Sorceress. They all held on and pulled.

The other Demons flew over to help Zip. Zip held
out the Book of Shadows for them to grab. Just then
Squig and Dorrie and the Great Sorceress and the
Big Witch gave a big tug. They pulled the broomstick right out from under him. Zane and Zeno
caught him, but the Book of Shadows dropped down
onto the balcony.

With angry screeches, the Demons fled into the darkness.

Dorrie and the Great Sorceress and the Big Witch and Squig all landed in a heap on the balcony. Squig was still holding tight to Zip's broomstick.

As they untangled themselves, a great hurrah rose from the courtyard.

"Thank you, my dear," said the Great Sorceress, as Dorrie helped her into her chair. "What a narrow escape! And who is this Mystery Witch who saved me?"

"The Mystery Witch! The Mystery Witch! Three cheers for the Mystery Witch!" everyone shouted.

"She looks very, very old," said the Big Witch.

"For an old lady she is very, very strong. She kicks like a horse!" said Squig.

"It's me, Dorrie," said Dorrie. "My mask shrank when we hit Black Pond, and the costume got all wet and muddy."

"Dorrie!" cried the Big Witch. "Shrank? Black Pond? The Demons tried to drown you!" She turned pale.

"No, no, I flew into the pond all by myself. The Demons didn't come until after I was stuck in a tree and. . . ."

The Great Sorceress put her hand on Dorrie's arm. "Never mind. You were in the right place at the right time, and that is what matters."

Dorrie looked at the Great Sorceress. The Great Sorceress winked. "Now someone bring me a cup of hot tea, please, and we will have a little magic."

Squig brought a cup of hot tea to the Sorceress. Everyone crowded around to watch.

"Just hold your face over the cup, Dorrie, while I hum a magic hum," said the Sorceress.

Dorrie felt the mask begin to stretch and sag. She lifted her head and pulled the mask off. She sneezed.

"Come along with me," said the Sorceress, getting up. "The band can play while we find you a dry costume."

Dorrie and Gink went with the Sorceress into her bedroom. She opened a big closet and began to pull out costumes.

"What were you before you became a Mystery Witch?" asked the Great Sorceress.

"A little princess," said Dorrie. "Cook is the castle, and Mother is the knight."

The Great Sorceress laughed. "A little princess, eh? We can do better than that. Let me see, you could be a ghost and haunt the castle. Or a jester."

"Oh, I'd like to be a jester," said Dorrie. "I like to do somersaults and cartwheels." She began pulling off the wet dress. The Sorceress helped her.

"Look," said the Sorceress. "There's something in the pocket." She pulled out a soggy piece of paper and unfolded it.

"This is the missing recipe from the Book of Shadows!" cried the Great Sorceress. "The Big Witch lost it years ago!"

"What does it do?" said Dorrie, getting into the jester's suit.

"It makes things invisible," said the Sorceress. "The Big Witch was learning to fly. There was a big table full of pumpkin pies all ready for the Halloween party. She crashed into the whole row of pies. She got the recipe to try to make herself invisible. The recipe disappeared, but the Big Witch didn't."

"Well," said Dorrie, "I feel better about the clothesline."

The Sorceress looked at her. "The clothesline?"

Dorrie told her what had happened with the broomstick.

They went out on the balcony. The band stopped playing. The Great Sorceress held up the Book and said:

"The lost recipe is found. The Book of Shadows is complete!"

While everyone clapped, Dorrie helped the Sorceress into the chair. And then she and Gink ran to join the others. The Pageant began.

Mr. Obs and Squig went on first, dancing and playing music. Six witches and wizards in black tights came leaping behind them as acrobats.

The Witch Doctor came next on a big bicycle. Miss Dorp skipped behind him, dressed as a pumpkin. Cook as a castle came after her, with the Big Witch as a knight marching beside her. All around them Dorrie did cartwheels and somersaults.

On and on they went, around and around the courtyard in the glow of the lighted pumpkins. There were all kinds of costumes. The Egg Witch was dressed as a chicken. There were clowns and devils, ghosts and dragons. There were playing cards and a big orange bug.

They all stopped below the balcony. Squig read a Halloween poem while Mr. Obs played his violin.

The Great Sorceress thanked them. She reached behind the chair and brought out Zip's broomstick. She came down into the courtyard and handed the broomstick to Dorrie.

"For our Mystery Witch!" said the Great Sorceress. Everybody clapped and cheered. "And I will give you flying lessons myself. I taught the Big Witch to fly, and I'll teach you. We'll start tomorrow at three o'clock."

"Oh, thank you," said Dorrie. And she smiled and smiled.

They had a big Halloween party in the courtyard. There were bowls of orange punch, and pumpkin cakes and pumpkin cookies and pumpkin pies.

When it was all over, the Great Sorceress gave each of them a lighted pumpkin. Up, up, up into the air they flew. The pumpkins shone like stars against the sky.

Dorrie went to bed with the broomstick right beside her. The Big Witch gave her a big kiss and blew out the candle. Gink yawned and curled up at Dorrie's feet.

One by one the pumpkins winked out all over Witchdom.